For my Honey, my babies and my Mummy.

In a tiny little house,
In a town by the shore
Lived four quite special children
One, two, three and four.

Kyle and Dylan were the oldest
And Sophie was their sis.

Then there was Cody and he was like this..
A climber and a clamberer. A giggler and maybe.....?

The NAUGHTIEST and CHEEKIEST of all the cheeky
babies!

For Cody was so troublesome, he made his parents grumble.
They never knew what to expect from their bodacious bundle.

He could escape from anywhere if he was in a rage.
His Mum and Dad thought they might have to keep him in a cage!
He hid all of their precious things, he tormented the cats,
He threw his food all on the floor with a huge gigantic splat!

He grizzled in his buggy!

He screamed in his car seat!

He wriggled down his high
chair and landed on his feet!

He nibbled on the cat's food!

He scribbled on the wall!

Mum says it's a wonder, Dad has any hair at all!

But Cody's big adventure was about to be much more.
As one morning, when he woke up, he found a special door!

This door was very different from the big one with the mat…
You see this was a special door, just for Cody's cats!
But Cody felt quite jealous that the cats had such a door.
If only *he* had such a thing so then he could explore!

So he made the tough decision, he and his toys would play outside
But that isn't where it ended and that wasn't all he'd hide…

Mummy's posh mascara…Daddy's aerosol…
His brother's English homework…his sister's Barbie doll
His family just couldn't guess where all their things had gone.
And Cody thought he'd had his fun but he was very wrong…

As strange things started happening, clues Cody couldn't crack.
The cats were going out a lot and bringing strange things back!
It started with a fossil and then some Roman stuff.
Then it was a helmet and a Tudor ruff.
Just last week the cats had strolled right through their little door
With linen on their tails and sand across the floor.

Now Cody was quite curious about the things he'd seen,
The explanation was quite clear....The cat flap's a...

TIME MACHINE!

The cats are going back in history, exploring ancient times.
Cody would have to go with them
So out he'd have to climb.

So he wriggled past the sofa, he toddled in a line.
He squeezed through the cat flap and appeared in ROMAN times.

Now everything was very strange and Cody thought now, maybe?
Ancient Rome was not the place for such a little baby.
"I miss my Mum, I miss my Dad," exclaimed the little Tot.
"I wonder if the cat flap works the other way or not?"

And just like that, strange arms began appearing right in Rome,
and pulled him right back through the void, and he was safe at home.
The arms belonged to Dylan, who was looking rather cross.
"Mum told me to watch you Codes, and you just wandered off!"

But Cody hadn't had enough, you could say he was hooked
So, he waited until bedtime and he hoped nobody looked.

As he.......wriggled past the sofa, he toddled in a line.
He squeezed through the cat flap
And appeared in **NORMAN** times!

And now he knew he could get home, he thought he should explore.
He heard a great big CLATTER BANG and headed to the shore.
It was there he found a battle and things were getting hairy.
But then an arm appeared before this place got far too scary.

The arm belonged to Sophie,
who yelled "What did you do that for?"
"If you keep climbing out of there,
We'll have to lock the door!"

But Cody would not stand for that, it made him rather glum.
He didn't want to get told off but was having too much fun!

So he....
Wriggled past the sofa, toddled in a line
He squeezed through the cat flap....WAIT!

He didn't get through easily, it seemed to take a while.
There was something holding on to him...it was his brother Kyle!

They'd BOTH gone through the cat flap,
Kyle had tried to stop his crimes
But the baby brought his brother back into the Tudor times!

Now Tudor times were dangerous.
They had to get back home!
But who was left to rescue them?
Would they be left alone?

Back at home and all was quiet, and had been for a while.
It was shocking how the house could change without Cody and Kyle.
The kids looked at the cat flap, then they looked at each other.
"We've got to go and rescue them, we've got to save our brothers!"

So they wriggled past the sofa,
They toddled in a line.
They squeezed through the cat flap
And appeared in 𝕿𝖚𝖉𝖔𝖗 times!

But they hadn't thought their journey through,
And they'd made the fat King shout.
They needed to get back home quick
But who would help them out?

Then suddenly before their eyes,
Their cats mewed "follow us!"
"We know the way, we'll get you home, before you make a fuss!"

So they all squeezed through the cat flap and they landed on their bums.
They prayed that they had not woken their daddy and their mum.
They *nearly* got into trouble and Cody thought now maybe...
Time travelling is just for cats and not a little baby.

So next time you see a cat flap,
Think of these little rhymes.
And don't wriggle, toddle and don't squeeze
Or you may get stuck in time!

Printed in Great Britain
by Amazon